D1549452

This book belongs to

....

Walt Disney's

Snow White and the Seven Dwarfs

Storybook Favourites

Reader's Digest Young Families

Walt Disney's Snow White and the Seven Dwarfs

Illustrations by The Walt Disney Studios
Story adapted by Jane Werner
Illustrations adapted by Campbell Grant

Once upon a time, in a faraway land, a lovely queen sat by her window, sewing. As she worked, she pricked her finger with her needle. Three drops of blood fell on the snow-white linen.

How happy I would be if I had a little girl with lips as red as blood, skin as white as snow, and hair as black as ebony, thought the Queen.

When spring came, her wish was granted. A little daughter was born to the Queen, and she was all her mother had desired. But the Queen's happiness was brief. Holding her lovely baby in her arms, she whispered, 'Little Snow White!' and then she died.

When the lonely King married again, his new queen was beautiful, but, alas, she was also heartless and cruel. She was jealous of all the lovely ladies in the kingdom, but most jealous of the lovely little princess – Snow White.

Now the evil Queen's most treasured possession was a magic mirror. Every day she looked into it and asked:

'Magic Mirror on the wall,
Who is the fairest one of all?'

If the Magic Mirror replied that she was the fairest in the land, all was well. But if another lady was named, the Queen flew into a terrible rage.

As the years passed, Snow White grew more and more beautiful, and her sweet nature made everyone love her – everyone but the Queen.

The Queen's chief fear was that Snow White might grow up to be the fairest in the land. So she banished the young princess to the servants' quarters, made her dress in rags, and forced her to work from morning to night.

But while she worked, Snow White dreamed dreams of a handsome prince who would come some day and carry her off to his castle in the clouds. And as she dusted and scrubbed – and dreamed – Snow White grew more beautiful day by day.

At last came the day the Queen had been dreading. She asked:

'Magic Mirror on the wall,
Who is the fairest one of all?'

And the Magic Mirror replied:

'Her lips blood red, her hair like night,
Her skin like snow, her name – Snow White!'

Pale with anger, the Queen rushed from the room and called the Huntsman to her.

'Take the princess into the forest and bring back her heart in a jewelled box,' she said sternly.

The Huntsman bowed his head in grief. He had no choice but to obey the cruel Queen's commands.

Snow White had no fear of the kindly Huntsman. She went happily into the forest with him. It was beautiful there among the trees, and the princess, not knowing what was in store for her, skipped along beside the Huntsman, stopping to pick violets and singing a happy tune.

At last, the poor Huntsman could bear it no longer. He fell to his knees before the princess.

'I cannot kill you, Princess,' he said, 'even though it is the Queen's command. Run into the forest and hide, and never return to the castle.'

Then away went the Huntsman. On his way back to the castle, he killed a small animal and took its heart in the jewelled box to the wicked Queen.

Alone in the forest, Snow White wept with fright. Deeper and deeper into the woods she ran, half-blinded by tears. It seemed to her that the roots of trees reached up to trip her, and that branches grabbed at her dress as she passed.

At last, weak with terror, Snow White fell to the ground and lay there, sobbing her heart out.

Ever so quietly, out from burrows and nests and hollow trees, crept the little woodland animals. Bunnies and chipmunks, and raccoons and squirrels gathered around to keep watch over her.

When Snow White looked up and saw them there, she smiled through her tears. At the sight of her smile, the little animals crept closer, snuggling in her lap or nestling in her arms. The birds sang their sweetest melodies, and the little forest clearing was filled with joy.

'I feel ever so much better now,' Snow White told her new friends, 'but I do still need a place to sleep.'

One of the birds chirped something, and the little animals nodded in agreement. Then away flew the birds, leading the way. The bunnies, chipmunks, raccoons and squirrels scampered after them, and Snow White followed.

At last, through a tangle of brush, Snow White saw a tiny cottage nestled in a clearing up ahead.

'How sweet!' she cried. 'It's just like a doll's house.' Snow White clapped her hands in delight.

Skipping across a little bridge to the house, Snow White peeped in through one windowpane. There seemed to be no one at home, but the sink was piled high with cups and saucers and plates, which looked as if they had never been washed. Dirty little shirts and wrinkled little trousers hung over chairs, and everything was covered with dust.

'Maybe the children who live here have no mother,' said Snow White, 'and need someone to take care of them. Let's clean their house and surprise them.'

So in she went, followed by her forest friends. Snow White found an old broom in the corner and swept the floor, while the little animals did their best to help.

Then Snow White washed all the crumpled little clothes, and set a pot of delicious soup to cook over the fire.

'Now,' she said to the animals, 'let's see what is upstairs.' Upstairs they found seven little beds in a row.

'Why, they have their names carved on them,' said Snow White. 'Doc, Happy, Sneezy, Dopey – such funny names for children! Grumpy, Bashful, Sleepy! My, I'm a little sleepy myself!'

Yawning, she lay down across the little beds and fell asleep. Quietly, the little animals stole away, and the birds flew out the window. All was still in the little house in the forest.

Seven little men came marching through the woods, singing on their way. As they came in sight of their cottage, they stopped short. Smoke was curling from the chimney, and the door was standing open!

'Look! Someone's in our house!' one cried. 'Maybe a ghost – er, a goblin – er, a demon!'

'I knew it,' said another, with a grumpy look. 'Been warning you for 200 years that something awful was about to happen!'

At last, on timid tiptoe, in they went.

'Someone's stolen our dishes,' growled the grumpy one.

'No, they're hidden in the cupboard,' said Happy with a grin. 'But, hey! My cup's been washed! Sugar's all gone!'

At that moment, a sound came from upstairs. It was Snow White yawning and turning in her sleep.

'It's up there – the goblin – er, demon – er, ghost!' exclaimed one Dwarf.

With their pickaxes on their shoulders, up the stairs they went – seven frightened little Dwarfs.

Standing in a row at the foot of their beds, they stared at the sleeping Snow White.

'Wh – what is it?' whispered one.

'It's mighty purty,' said another.

'Why, bless my soul, I think it's a girl!' said a third.

And then Snow White woke up. 'Why, you're not children!' she exclaimed. 'You're little men. Let me see if I can guess your names.' And she did – all of them.

She went down and looked at the soup cooking on the fire. 'Supper's not quite ready,' said Snow White. 'You'll have just enough time to wash.'

'Wash!' cried the little men, with horror in their voices. They hadn't washed for, oh, it seemed hundreds of years. But out they marched when Snow White insisted. And it was worth it in the end. For they had never tasted such a supper. Nor had they ever had such an evening of fun. All the forest folk gathered around the cottage windows to watch them play and dance and sing.

Meanwhile, back at the castle, the Huntsman had presented to the wicked Queen the box which, she thought, held Snow White's heart.

'Aha!' she cried. 'At last!' And down the castle corridors she hurried straight to the Magic Mirror and she asked:

'Magic Mirror on the wall,
Who is the fairest one of all?'

But the Magic Mirror replied:

'With the Seven Dwarfs will spend the night
The fairest in the land, Snow White.'

Then the Queen realised that the Huntsman had tricked her. She flung the jewelled box at the Magic Mirror, shattering the glass into a thousand pieces. Then, shaking with rage, the Queen hurried down to a dark cave below the palace where she worked her black magic.

First, she disguised herself as a toothless old woman dressed in tattered rags. Then, she searched through her books of magic spells for a horrid spell to cast on Snow White.

'What shall it be?' she muttered to herself. 'The poisoned apple, the Sleeping Death? Perfect!'

In a great kettle she stirred up a poison brew. Then she dipped an apple into it – one, two, three times – and the apple came out a beautiful rosy red, the most tempting apple you could hope to see.

Cackling with wicked pleasure, the Queen dropped a poisoned apple into a basket of fruit and started on her journey to the home of the Seven Dwarfs.

She felt certain that her plan would succeed, for the magic spell of the Sleeping Death could be broken only by Love's First Kiss.

And the Queen was certain that no one would find Snow White asleep in that great forest.

It was morning when the Queen reached the great forest, close to the Dwarfs' cottage. From her hiding place she saw Snow White saying goodbye to the Seven Dwarfs as they marched off to work.

'Now, be careful!' they warned her. 'Watch out for the Queen.' And Snow White promised that she would.

But when the poor, ragged old woman carrying a basket of apples appeared outside her window, Snow White never thought to be afraid. She gave the old woman a drink of water and spoke to her kindly.

'Thank you, my dear,' the Queen cackled. 'Now, in return, won't you have one of my beautiful apples?' And she held out the poisoned fruit to Snow White.

Down swooped the little birds and animals, pecking and clawing at the wicked Queen. But still Snow White did not understand. 'Stop it!' she cried. 'Shame on you.' Then she took the poisoned apple and bit into it, and fell down lifeless on the cottage floor.

Away went the frantic birds and animals into the woods to warn the Seven Dwarfs. Now, the Dwarfs had decided among themselves not to do their usual jobs that day. Away at their mine, they were hard at work making a special gift for Snow White.

They looked up in surprise as the birds and animals crowded around them. At first, they did not understand. Then, they realised that Snow White must be in danger. 'The Queen!' they cried, and ran for home.

They were too late. They raced into the clearing just in time to see the Queen slip away into the shadows. They chased her through the woods until she plunged into a bottomless gulf and disappeared forever. But it didn't bring Snow White back to life.

When the Dwarfs returned home, they found Snow White lying on the floor as if asleep.

They built her a bed of crystal and gold, and set it up in the forest. There they kept watch, night and day.

After a time, the handsome Prince of a nearby kingdom heard travellers tell of the lovely princess asleep in the forest, and he rode there to see her. At once he knew that he loved her truly, so he knelt beside her and kissed her lips.

At the touch of Love's First Kiss, Snow White awoke. There, bending over her, was the Prince of her dreams. Snow White knew that she loved him, too. She said goodbye to the Seven Dwarfs and, on a white horse, rode off with the Prince to his Castle of Dreams Come True.